S A
TOY PANDA

84

KNOWLEDGE BOOKS

MASTERY DECODABLES

Tas likes her toy panda.

Tas likes her toy rabbit.

Ted is her toy panda.

Babbit is her toy rabbit.

Ted panda likes to sleep.

Babbit the rabbit likes to sleep.

zzZ
zzZ

Babbit the rabbit is small.

Ted the panda is big.

Tas likes Babbit and Ted.

Tas likes to sleep.

ZZZ

Ted likes to sleep.

Babbit likes to sleep.

ZZZ

Tas likes to sit.

Ted likes to sit.

Babbit likes to sit.

Can Babbit hop? Yes, yes, yes!

Can Ted hop? No, no no!

Can Tas sing? Yes, yes, yes!

Can Ted sing? Yes, yes, yes!

Tas likes Ted and Babbit.